The T....
Little Kitten

by **Barbara Shook Hazen** • illustrated by **Jan Pfloog**

Originally published as The Tiny, Tawny Kitten

g **A GOLDEN BOOK • NEW YORK**

Golden Books Publishing Company, Inc., New York, New York 10106

Once there was a tiny, tawny kitten. She had eyes
the color of bluebells, and her tail and paws were
tipped with white. The tiny, tawny kitten was afraid
of everything. She even backed away from beetles.

She leaped from her sunny window sill
whenever a large beady-eyed pigeon
decided to land on the ledge outside.

She was even afraid of her own shadow. She jumped
when she saw it moving along the garden wall. Quickly,
the tiny, tawny kitten scampered back to her little girl.

"Silly kitten, you mustn't be afraid of everything,"
the little girl said. "I want you to grow up to be a big,
brave tiger cat. And you will—someday."

The tiny, tawny kitten liked things that were little like herself.

She liked to lap milk from a small dish.

She liked to curl up in a small basket.

She liked her little piece of string and her little catnip mouse. They were just right for tiny kitten games.

The tiny kitten did not like big things. She did not like big boys on bikes or big yapping dogs. She did not like big trucks that rattled down the street.

The tiny, tawny kitten did not even like big cats.
Sometimes a fat-faced Persian named Miranda came
over the wall to sun herself in the kitten's yard.
Miranda had a long, feathery tail, very sharp claws,
and a shrill meow.

The tiny kitten did not want that fat, sassy cat to take over her yard. When Miranda was nearby, the tiny kitten hid under the hollyhocks. She did not come out even when Miranda chewed the tail off the catnip mouse. The tiny kitten was afraid.

At night the alley cats scrambled over the
fence. They sat on the garbage cans and on
the garden wall. They meowed to the moon
and sang to each other. The tiny, tawny kitten
watched from the window. She watched the
lean, lanky alley cats, the spotted meat market
cat, the large, gray rat-catcher cat, and the
striped firehouse cat. And the tiny, tawny
kitten was afraid.

But the tiny, tawny kitten was most afraid of Old Ebenezer, the big hound that lived next door.

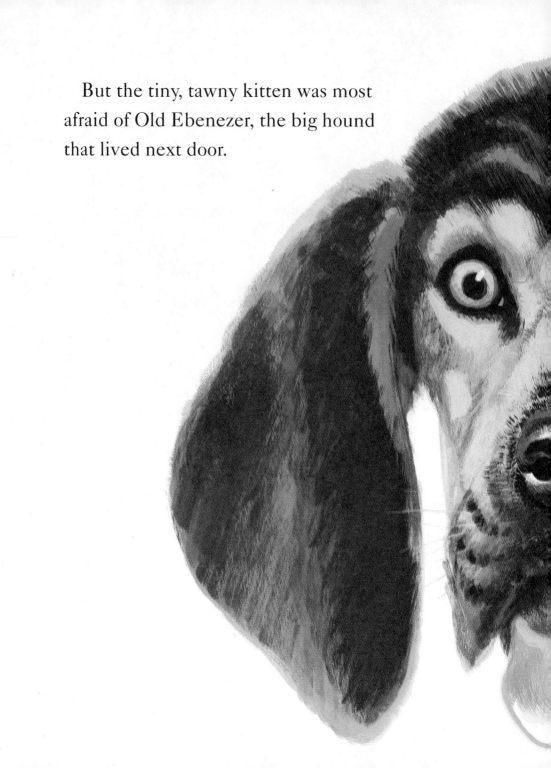

One day the kitten was sitting in her yard when . . . suddenly, she heard something moving through the grass. There was Ebenezer, three feet away!

The tiny, tawny kitten was very, very frightened.
She arched her back and bristled her fur. She
began to hiss and spit and meorrrowww!

Suddenly, an amazing thing happened. The tiny, tawny kitten sprang forward and smacked Ebenezer in the face with her tiny paw! Then another amazing thing happened. Old Ebenezer yelped, and ran away!

From that day on, the tiny, tawny kitten grew braver. Ebenezer was large and noisy, yet he had run when she faced him bravely, like a real tiger cat.

And that is what the tiny, tawny kitten grew up to be—a big, brave tiger cat, just as the little girl said she would.